Wee Sing®
Musical Bible

PSS!
PRICE STERN SLOAN

_____

Presented to

_____

on

God's CREATION

Genesis 1

God made the whole world. He made the flowers and the trees and the water and the stars. God made the sun so we can have daylight. The sun makes us warm when we are outside on sunny days. God is good. Everything he made is good.

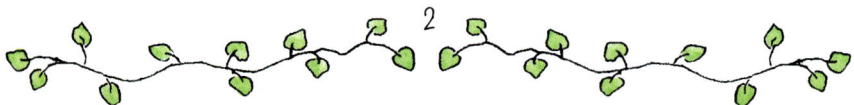

Who made ocean, earth, and sky? God, our loving Father ...

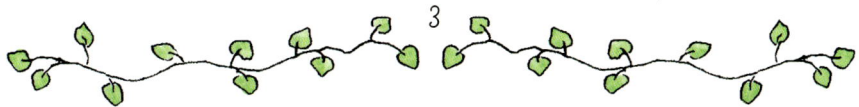

Bible Verse

In the beginning
God created
the heavens
and the earth.

Genesis 1:1

My Prayer

Dear God, thank you
for making a beautiful
world for me to live in.
You are wonderful!

Amen.

5

God Made PEOPLE

Genesis 1-2

Adam and Eve were the very first man and woman. God made them. He gave them a beautiful place to live called the Garden of Eden. They were very happy.

God made the animals, too.

God made me; God made me;

in my Bible book it says that God made me . . .

Bible Verse

God created
people in his
own image.

Genesis 1:27

8

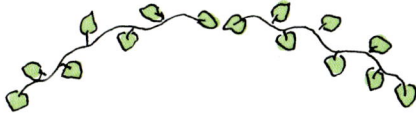

My Prayer

Dear God,
thank you
so much for
making me special.
Amen.

Noah's BOAT

Genesis 6

God told Noah to build a huge boat called an ark. Noah's sons helped him. The ark was not in the water. But soon it began to rain and rain until there was water everywhere. Noah and his family and two of every animal were safe in the boat.

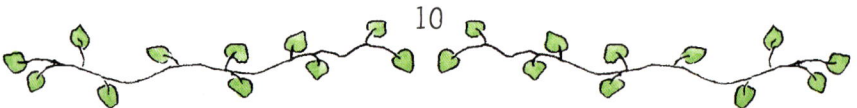

Who built the ark? Noah! Noah! . . .

Bible Verse

Noah did everything
exactly as God had
commanded him.

Genesis 6:22

My Prayer

Dear God, thank you for keeping Noah safe. Please keep me safe, too. I love you.

Amen.

Baby MOSES

Exodus 2

Look what the princess found in the river! She found a baby boy floating in a basket. She named him Moses. Some men wanted to kill the baby. God sent the princess to find the baby Moses and take care of him.

Silently sleep, baby, safely sleep,

for God will take care of you...

Bible Verse

The Lord keeps

watch over you.

Psalm 121:8

My Prayer

Dear God, I love you.
I'm glad you love me,
too. I'm glad you take
good care of me.
Thank you!
Amen.

The Burning BUSH

Exodus 3

When Moses grew up, he took care of
sheep. One day he saw a bush on fire, but
he didn't know why it didn't burn up. Then
he knew why—because God was there!
God spoke to Moses from the bush. God
said, "Go and help my people." Moses was
afraid at first, but God said he would help
Moses.

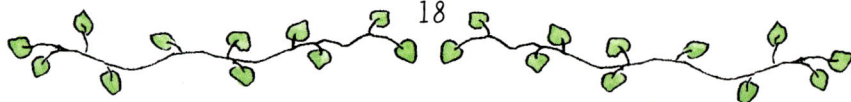

When I work or play, God is with me; I don't have to worry anymore...

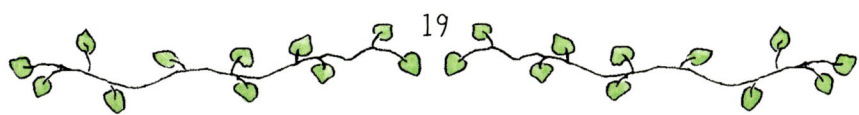

Bible Verse

God said,

"I will be with you."

Exodus 3:12

My Prayer

Lord, I feel safe
when I think about you.
Help me remember
that you are always
with me. Thank you.
Amen.

God's
POWER

Exodus 14

God's people were afraid. They were escaping from a mean king. They were standing at the edge of a big lake called the Red Sea. Can you see the water standing up along both sides? When Moses held up his stick, God made the water open up. Then the people walked on dry ground through the lake.

How great is our God, forever the same!
He rolled back the waters of the mighty Red Sea...

Bible Verse

Moses answered,
"Don't be afraid! Stand
still and see the Lord
save you today."

Exodus 14:13

My Prayer

Dear God, thank you
for true stories about
real people like Moses.
I love to learn how
you help your people.
Amen.

God's
RULES

Exodus 20

Moses listened to God. God told Moses ten very
important rules he wants his people to obey. God
wrote these ten rules on pieces of stone.

These rules are called the Ten Commandments.

Trust and obey—there's no other way;

all his commands he gives for our own good . . .

Bible Verse

Give me understanding

so I can learn your

commands.

Psalm 119:73

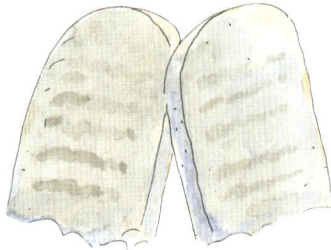

My Prayer

Dear God,

please help me

obey your rules.

Thanks for knowing

what's best for me.

Amen.

Victory at JERICHO

Joshua 6

Joshua was a leader of God's people. God told him to take over the town of Jericho. He told Joshua just how to do it. Joshua obeyed God. He and all the people walked around the walls. They blew their trumpets and shouted. Then all the walls fell down and God's people went into the town!

Joshua fought the battle of Jericho,
and the walls came tumbling down...

31

Bible Verse

The Lord

was with

Joshua.

Joshua 6:27

My Prayer

Dear God,
thank you for being
with Joshua.
I'm glad that
you're with me, too.
Amen.

Strong
SAMSON

Judges 15

Samson was a very, very strong man. See how easily he broke the ropes! Once he killed a lion with his bare hands. Another time he knocked down a palace to punish God's enemies. God made him strong so he could help God's people.

Be strong in the Lord and in His mighty power . . .

Bible Verse

Be strong
with the Lord's
mighty power.

Ephesians 6:10

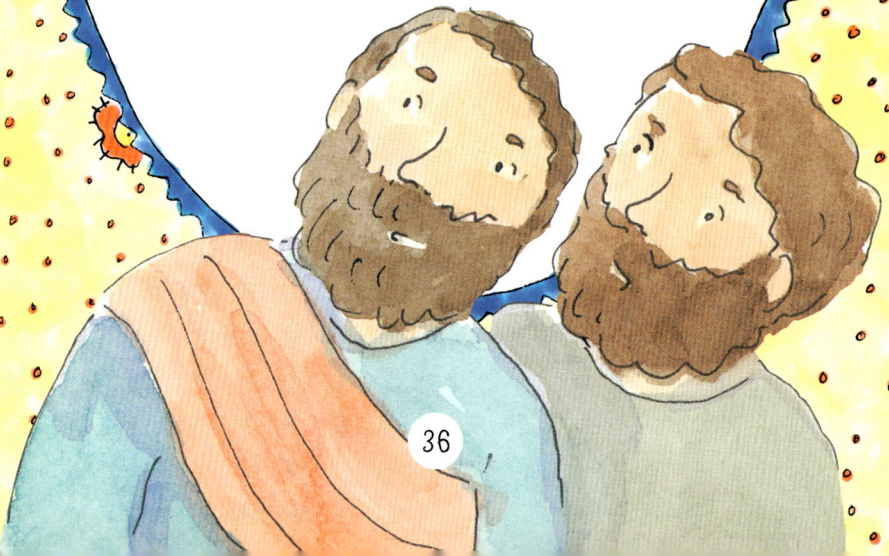

My Prayer

Lord, I'm glad
you make me strong.
I want to be strong
so I can be
a good helper.
Thank you, God.
Amen.

Ruth and NAOMI

Ruth 1

Naomi felt sad because her husband and sons had died. Ruth had been married to one of those sons. She wanted to help Naomi feel better. She decided to stay with Naomi and help her.

God wants us to be helpers, too.

People are hungry—I can help. People are lonely—I can help . . .

Bible Verse

Ruth replied . . . "I will go wherever you go and live wherever you live."

Ruth 1:16

My Prayer

Dear God, I'm glad
you let me be a helper.
Thank you for the people
who help me, too.
Thanks for caring.
Amen.

David's SONGS

1 Samuel 16

David was a special friend of God. When he was a boy, he took care of his father's sheep. Can you see him playing his harp? David wrote beautiful songs to tell God that he loved him. Many of his songs are in the Bible. They are called psalms.

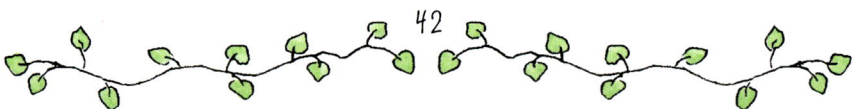

Little David play on your harp; hallelu, hallelu . . .

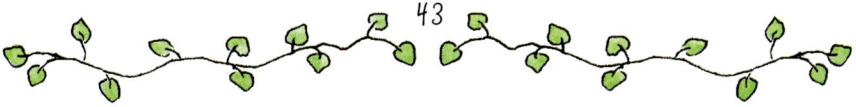

Bible Verse

I will praise you

with songs of joy.

Psalm 63:5

My Prayer

Dear God, I'm thankful
for music and musical
instruments. I like to
sing praises to you,
just like David!
Amen.

David's SHEEP

1 Samuel 17

David was a shepherd. That means he took care of sheep. He took good care of them. This lion wanted to eat David's sheep. With God's help David killed the lion so it couldn't hurt the sheep.

God is *your* shepherd. He takes good care of you.

The Lord is my shepherd;

I'll walk with him always . . .

Bible Verse

The Lord is my
shepherd. I have
everything I need.

Psalm 23:1

My Prayer

Dear God,
thank you for
taking good care
of me.
Amen.

David and GOLIATH

1 Samuel 17

Goliath was a giant who wanted to hurt God's people with his spear and sword. David used his slingshot to throw a stone at the giant. David knew God would help him. The stone hit Goliath, and he fell down. He didn't get up again. God's people were safe from that mean giant.

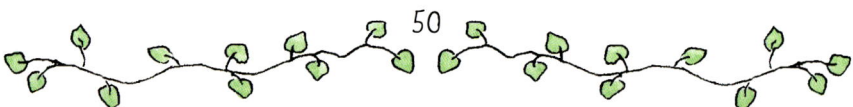

Only a boy named David, only a little sling...

Bible Verse

If God is for us,

who can be

against us?

Romans 8:31

52

My Prayer

Dear God,

I'm not very big,

but I know

you'll always

help me.

Amen.

David
DANCES

2 Samuel 6

David grew up to be the king of Israel. The big golden box behind him had God's Ten Commandments inside.

When David brought this beautiful box to Jerusalem, he jumped for joy. He loved God, and God loved him.

God loves you, too. You should be very happy.

Rejoice in the Lord always, and again I say rejoice! ...

Bible Verse

Rejoice in the Lord always.

Philippians 4:4

My Prayer

Thank you, God,

for loving me.

I like to sing and

shout my love to you!

I'm glad you want

my praises.

Amen.

Wise
SOLOMON

1 Kings 1

David had a son named Solomon. God's helper, Nathan, put his hands on Solomon's head to make him the next king. Solomon asked God to make him a wise king. He wanted to know how to do what was right. God was pleased with Solomon and made him very wise.

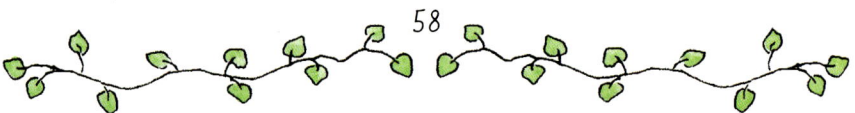

The wise man built his house upon the rock....

Bible Verse

Solomon answered . . .

"I ask that

you give me wisdom."

1 Kings 3:6-9

My Prayer

Dear God, I want to be wise. I want to know what the Bible says about pleasing you. Amen.

Jonah and the WHALE

Jonah 1-3

Jonah didn't want to obey God. He tried to run away by getting on a boat, but God sent a storm. Some men on the boat threw Jonah into the water. A whale swallowed him. Jonah talked to God from inside the whale. He told God how sorry he was. After three days the whale spit Jonah out onto the sand. Then Jonah obeyed God.

Who did swallow Jonah, who did swallow Jonah down? . . .

63

Bible Verse

I will obey

your word.

Psalm 119:17

My Prayer

Dear God, I'm sorry
when I don't obey.
Help me to not run
away from the things
I'm supposed to do.
Amen.

Daniel and the LIONS

Daniel 6

Daniel prayed to God. He would not pray to anyone else—not even the king. So the king's helpers were angry. They put Daniel into a lion's den. They thought the lions would eat him. But God sent an angel to keep Daniel safe. The lions could not open their mouths. They could not hurt Daniel.

Dare to be a Daniel; dare to stand alone! ...

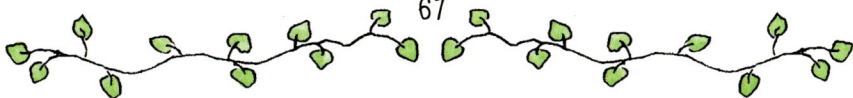

Bible Verse

Stand true to what you

believe. Be courageous.

Be strong.

1 Corinthians 16:13

68

My Prayer

Dear God, no one
is more important
than you. Teach me to
always put you first
in my life.
Amen.

Gabriel's VISIT

Luke 1

The angel Gabriel came to tell Mary something very important. He told her that God would bless her and make her the mother of God's Son! Mary was very excited! She was happy because she would be the mother of the Savior. When the baby was born, she named him Jesus.

I'm happy to hear—
happy to hear the angel's holy words...

Bible Verse

Mary said, "I am the servant girl of the Lord. Let this happen to me as you say!"

Luke 1:38

72

My Prayer

Dear God, thank you
for sending your Son,
Jesus, into the world.
Thank you for giving
him a good mother
like Mary.
Amen.

Mary's BABY

Luke 2

Mary had a baby. His name is Jesus! He was a great king in heaven before he came down to earth as a baby. He is God's Son, but he was born in a stable where sheep and donkeys live.

Away in a manger, no crib for a bed...

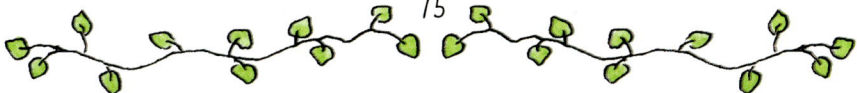

Bible Verse

[Mary] wrapped him
snugly in strips of cloth
and laid him in a manger.

Luke 2:7

76

My Prayer

Dear God, thank you for sending a very special Gift to the world—your very own Son, Jesus! Amen.

Shepherds and ANGELS

Luke 2

These shepherds were outside Bethlehem taking care of their sheep. Suddenly they saw an angel. He told them Jesus had been born in a stable in the town of Bethlehem. Later, many other angels came to the shepherds. They all praised God because he sent Jesus to save us.

There was one, there were two, there were three little angels...

Bible Verse

All the angels were

praising God.

Luke 2:13

My Prayer

Dear God,

I praise you,

just like the angels,

for sending

baby Jesus!

Amen.

Shepherds Visit
JESUS

Luke 2

The shepherds ran into the town of Bethlehem to find the baby. They found him in a stable, just as the angel had said. Jesus looked like any baby, but the shepherds knew he was God's Son. The angel had told them that Jesus came to be the Savior. Then they went back to their sheep, praising God. They were so happy they had found baby Jesus!

Go tell it on the mountain, over the hills and everywhere!...

83

Bible Verse

The shepherds said to each other, "Come on, let's go to Bethlehem! Let's see this wonderful thing that has happened."

Luke 2:15

My Prayer

Dear God, I'm so excited
about your Son, Jesus—
just like the shepherds
on the night
Jesus was born!
Amen.

Wise MEN

Matthew 2

Jesus and his mother had visitors. Some wise men from far away came with presents for Jesus. They saw a special star, and it led them to Jesus. They knew Jesus was special. That is why they brought him gifts.

We three kings of Orient are
bearing gifts, we traverse afar...

Bible Verse

When the wise men
saw the star, they
were filled with joy.

Matthew 2:10

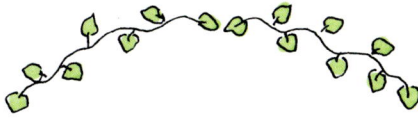

My Prayer

Dear Jesus, the wise men
didn't know much about
you, but they worshiped
you. I know a lot about
you, so of course I want
to worship you, too!
Amen.

Jesus at the TEMPLE

Luke 2

Jesus became a big boy. He turned twelve years old. He went to the Temple to talk with the leaders of God's people. They talked about very important things. Jesus surprised the leaders with his wise thoughts and good answers.

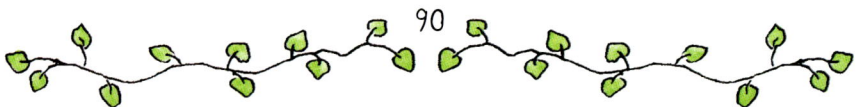

Lord Jesus, help me day by day to grow like you in every way...

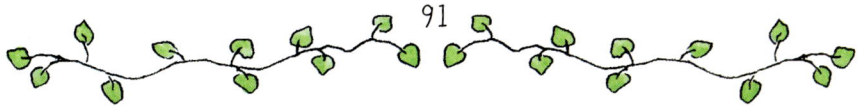

Bible Verse

Jesus continued to
learn more and more
and to grow.

Luke 2:52

My Prayer

Dear Jesus, please
help me to learn
many things. And help
me grow up
to be just like you.
Amen.

Jesus' FRIENDS

Matthew 4

Jesus liked talking with his friends. They were called his disciples. Some of them were fishermen, but Jesus wanted them to come with him instead. Soon they were telling people about God's love.

You can tell people about God's love, too.

94

He has called us, too. We are his disciples; I am one and you . . .

95

Bible Verse

"All people will know that you are my followers if you love each other."

John 13:35

My Prayer

Dear Jesus, I want
to follow you. I want
to help other people
follow you, too.
I want to tell them
that you love them.
Amen.

The Golden
RULE

Matthew 5-7

Jesus told the people about God. He said that God wants
us to be kind to everyone. He doesn't want us to quarrel.
Jesus told us: "Do to others what you would have them
do to you."

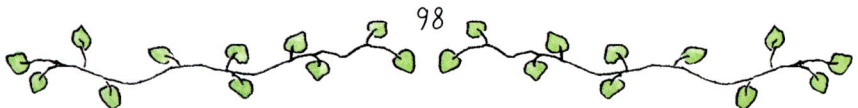

Do to others what you would have them do to you...

Bible Verse

"Do to others what
you would have them
do to you."

Matthew 7:12

My Prayer

Dear Jesus, thank you
for teaching me
the Golden Rule.
Help me try my best to
be kind to others.
Thank you, Jesus.
Amen.

A Boy's LUNCH

John 6

These people came to see Jesus. After a while, they became hungry. So a little boy shared his lunch with Jesus. Then Jesus made it become enough for everyone. It was a miracle! Jesus' helpers gave the food to many, many people.

Jesus can do lots of wonderful things like that!

Hallelu, hallelu, hallelu, hallelujah!

Praise ye the Lord! . . .

Bible Verse

Jesus . . . gave them as
much as they wanted.
They all had
enough to eat.

John 6:11 & 12

My Prayer

Dear Jesus, I praise you
for caring about
all those people.
I know you will
take care of me, too.
Amen.

The STORM

Luke 8

One day, Jesus and his friends were crossing a lake in a boat. Jesus lay down for a nap and was sleeping when a big storm came. His friends were scared because they thought the boat was going to sink. So they woke Jesus up. "We are all going to die!" they shouted. But Jesus stood up and told the storm to stop, and it did. Then Jesus asked his friends why they didn't trust him.

Deep, deep as the deepest sea is my Savior's love...

Bible Verse

Jesus got up and gave

a command to the wind

and the waves.

The wind stopped, and

the lake became calm.

Luke 8:24

My Prayer

Dear Jesus, thank you for being with me during storms and other times when I'm afraid. Help me to trust you.

Amen.

The Good
SHEPHERD

John 10

A shepherd takes good care
of his sheep. He looks for them
if they are lost. He picks up the
lambs if they are hurt. Jesus
said he is like a shepherd. We
are like sheep. Even though we
can't see him, we know he
takes care of us.

110

Be my shepherd; show me how to live my life for You . . .

Bible Verse

Jesus said . . . "I am the
good shepherd.
The good shepherd
lays down his life
for the sheep."

John 10:7-11

My Prayer

Dear Jesus, I'm so glad you're my good shepherd! Thank you for letting me be *your* little lamb.

Amen.

The Good
SAMARITAN

Luke 10

The man on the ground was badly hurt by robbers. Two people passed by and saw him, but they didn't help him. Then a kind person came along. He stopped and put bandages on the hurting man's cuts. The man who helped him was called the *Good Samaritan*. You can be a *Good Samaritan* by helping people.

Love, love, love, love—

Christians, this is your call . . .

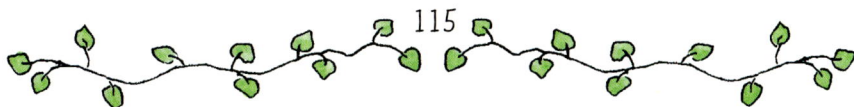

Bible Verse

Never get tired
of doing good.

2 Thessalonians 3:13

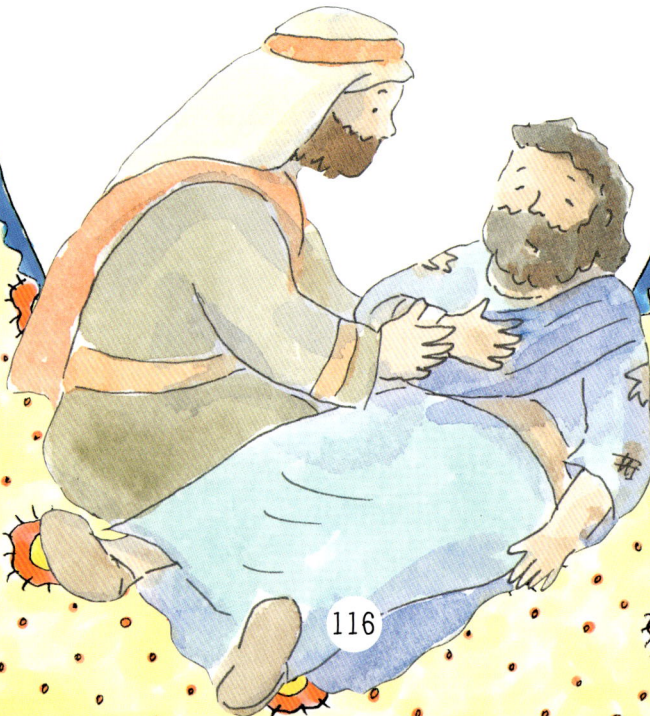

My Prayer

Dear God, I'm sad that people didn't care about the man who was hurt. But I'm glad that the Good Samaritan cared. I want to care about people, too.

Amen.

Martha and MARY

Luke 10

One day Jesus visited his friends Martha and Mary. Martha was busy cooking a big dinner. But her sister, Mary, sat down and listened to Jesus. Martha complained to Jesus because Mary wasn't helping her. Jesus didn't want Martha to be angry with her sister or worry too much about making a big meal. He wanted both Mary *and* Martha to take some time and listen to his teaching.

Listen to God say what is true.

Listen to God say what to do . . .

Bible Verse

Always be

willing to listen.

James 1:19

My Prayer

Dear Jesus,

I want to be close

to you. Help me listen

to you and always

put you first.

Amen.

The Little CHILDREN

Luke 18

Jesus loves children. Once some mothers brought their children to Jesus. Jesus' friends told them to go away. Jesus said, "No, let them come to me." Then Jesus held the children in his arms and loved them.

Jesus loves you, too.

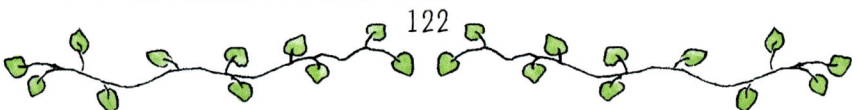

Jesus loves the little children—
all the children of the world...

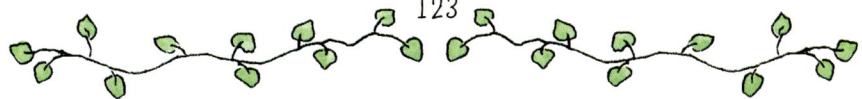

Bible Verse

"The kingdom of God
belongs to people
who are like
these little children."

Luke 18:16

My Prayer

Dear Jesus,

I'm glad that

I'm so special to you!

Amen.

ZACCHAEUS

Luke 19

Zacchaeus climbed a tree to see Jesus. Jesus stopped to talk to him. Jesus told him, "Come down because I am going to your house today." Zacchaeus was happy to meet Jesus. He was excited because he knew that Jesus was very special. He wanted Jesus to forgive him for the wrong things he had done.

"Zacchaeus, you come down, for I'm going to your house today . . ."

127

Bible Verse

[Jesus said,] "Here I am! I stand at the door and knock. If anyone hears my voice and opens the door, I will come in."

Revelation 3:20

My Prayer

Dear Jesus, please
be with me today.
I know you are with
me even if I can't
see you.
Amen.

HOSANNA!

John 12

Jesus came into town riding on a donkey. This little girl sang about how wonderful Jesus is. Many grown-ups and children waved palm branches to show that they were happy. They all wanted Jesus to be their new king.

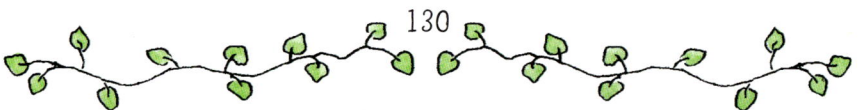

One of his heralds, yes, I would sing . . . loudest hosannas, "Jesus is King!" . . .

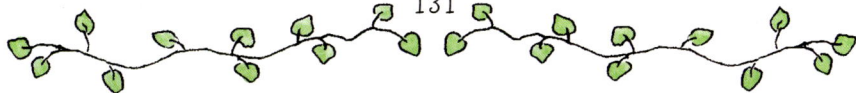

Bible Verse

I will praise the Lord

all my life.

Psalm 146:2

My Prayer

Dear Jesus, I would like to have waved a palm branch when you rode on a donkey. But I can still praise you and tell you that I love you. Amen.

A Thankful WOMAN

Luke 21

This woman was poor. She didn't have very much. But she was still thankful for all God had given her. He had taken care of her. By offering two very small coins, the woman showed God how thankful she was. She knew God would always help her have everything she needed.

Give, then, what you can give;

there is something all can give...

135

Bible Verse

Remember the words of the Lord Jesus: "It is more blessed to give than to receive."

Acts 20:35

136

My Prayer

Dear God, I'm so
thankful for all you've
given me. I want to give
you my love, my help,
and anything else I can
offer to you.

Amen.

Jesus
PRAYS

Luke 22

Jesus was praying. He knew he would soon die for our sins. He didn't want to die, but Jesus knew that God his Father would give him the courage he would need.

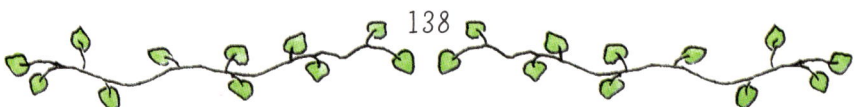

Christ came to save, his life he gave, to rescue you and me...

Bible Verse

[Jesus said,] "I have come to do your will, O God."

Hebrews 10:7

My Prayer

Dear Jesus,

I'm glad you did what

God, your Father in

heaven, wanted.

Amen.

The CROSS

Luke 23

Jesus died on a cross. He died so that we can have a new life. He died because he loves us. He loves us even though we have done wrong things. God sent his Son, Jesus, to take the blame for our sins.

144

Oh, how I love Jesus—because he first loved me...

143

Bible Verse

"God loved the world
so much that he gave
his only Son ... so that
whoever believes in him
may not be lost, but
have eternal life."

John 3:16

My Prayer

Dear Jesus,
thank you for giving
your life so that
God can forgive
the wrong things
I've done.

Amen.

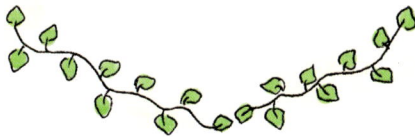

The Easter
STORY

Luke 24

After Jesus died, his friends put his body into a grave. A few days later, two women came and looked into the grave. But Jesus' body wasn't there! Then two angels came to the women and said, "Jesus is not here. He has risen from death!" The women hurried back to tell this exciting news to Jesus' friends.

Later, Jesus rose up in the sky and went back to heaven.

Sing Hallelujah! Sing Hallelujah!

My Jesus is alive forevermore . . .

Bible Verse

"Jesus is not here.

He has risen

from death!"

Luke 24:6

My Prayer

Dear Jesus, I'm so
glad that you came
back to life.
I know you're alive and
that you hear
my prayers!
Amen.

The BIBLE

Look at these little children—they are reading stories from the Bible. The Bible is also called God's Word. It tells us that God loves us very much. It tells us that God loves us so much that he gave us his only Son, Jesus.

The B-I-B-L-E . . . yes, that's the book for me! . . .

151

Bible Verse

The word of God
is full of living power.

Hebrews 4:12

My Prayer

Dear God, thank you for the Bible. It teaches me that you love me. Thank you for sending your Son, Jesus. I love you! Amen.

Bible Stories
and *Wee Sing* Songs

God's Creation
"God Our Loving Father"

God Made People
"God Made Me"

Noah's Boat
"Who Built the Ark?"

Baby Moses
"Baby Moses"

The Burning Bush
"God Is with Me"

God's Power
"How Great Is Our God"

God's Rules
"Trust and Obey"

Victory at Jericho
"Joshua Fought the Battle of Jericho"

Strong Samson
"Be Strong in the Lord"

Ruth and Naomi
"I Can Help"

David's Songs
"Little David, Play on Your Harp"

David's Sheep
"The Lord Is My Shepherd"

David and Goliath
"Only a Boy Named David"

David Dances
"Rejoice in the Lord Always"

Wise Solomon
"The Wise Man and Foolish Man"

Jonah and the Whale
"Who Did Swallow Jonah Down?"

Daniel and the Lions
"Dare to Be a Daniel"

Gabriel's Visit
"Happy to Be"

Mary's Baby
"Away in a Manger"

Shepherds and Angels
"Angel Band"

Shepherds Visit Jesus
"Go Tell It on the Mountain"

Wise Men
"We Three Kings"

Jesus at the Temple
"A Little Prayer"

Jesus' Friends
"There Were Twelve Disciples"

The Golden Rule
"The Golden Rule"

A Boy's Lunch
"Hallelu, Hallelu"

The Storm
"Wide, Wide Is the Ocean"

The Good Shepherd
"Be My Shepherd"

The Good Samaritan
"Love, Love (Round)"

Martha and Mary
"Listen to God"

The Little Children
"Jesus Loves the Little Children"

Zacchaeus
"Zacchaeus"

Hosanna!
"Tell Me the Stories of Jesus"

A Thankful Woman
"'Give,' Said the Little Stream"

Jesus Prays
"'Tis Simple as Can Be"

The Cross
"Oh, How I Love Jesus"

The Easter Story
"Alive, Alive"

The Bible
"The B-I-B-L-E"

LEADERS OF THOUGHT

IN THE MODERN CHURCH